HELLO

by

E. Hughes

Love-LovePublishing—Madison, WI
ISBN: 978-1-7334454-0-5
Title: *Hello*
Author: E. Hughes
Available Formats:
Paperback and eBook distribution

Other works by E. Hughes

Fiction:
Business as Usual
Disappear, Love
A Mediterranean Romance: The Capa Royals
The Sapphire Chronicles: Broken Lair
Infatuation
Beyond the Plain (Poetry)

Children's Books:
Penelope Helps Mom and Dad
Penelope: Be Kind to Animals
Penelope: Super Duper Spectacular Princess Ballerina

Nonfiction
Starting Your First Patio Garden: A Coffee Book
Family in a Time of Covid-19: The Truth about Coronavirus, How to Protect Yourself and Prepare

FADE IN:

EXT. DOWNTOWN CHICAGO (STATE & JACKSON) –
NIGHT

A man in a fedora and a beige London Fog
trench coat enters the stairway of a seamy
underground train platform.

INT. DOWNTOWN CHICAGO SUBWAY – CONTINUE

He descends the stairway and stops at a
rudimentary ticket kiosk, dips his ticket
into a slot, and pushes through the unlocked
three-bar wheel allowing him passage.

The platform is eerily quiet. Empty. Grey.
There, the only sign of life is a hollow wind,
like God's breath, blowing a sheet of newspaper
across the concrete into puddles of urine and
stagnant water. A sewer rat scrambles along the
train tracks.

TERENCE THORTON (30s, Black); crinkles his nose
and grunts in frustration of the stench.

He lights a cigarette: A quiet HISS before
he blows the match.

A nearby exit sign flickers then burns out in
the distance. For a moment, the underground
train station is enveloped in darkness.

A loud ROAR; an approaching train offers a
beam of salvation and steady light.

Terence pulls his trench coat closed as the
"B" train zooms by. He shakes his head

impatiently then looks at his watch. His cigarette, under the influence of gravity begins its descent from the corner of his mouth.

He checks the smoking appendage with his teeth, inhaling like an asthmatic.

Suddenly, a SHADOW looms beside him. He turns, stealing a glimpse of a STRANGER from the corner of his eye, staring directly into the barrel of a gun.

 Another ROAR: The "A" Train pulls into the station then stops. The doors open. Two oblivious passengers race from the stairway through the three-bar gate at the far end of the platform and climb aboard.

INT. TRAIN - CONTINUE

The STRANGER, whose face is unseen, finds a seat at the front of the cabin.
INT. DOWNTOWN CHICAGO SUBWAY - SAME

Terence stumbles into a phone booth with a bullet wound to the chest. He slides to the floor.

Blood gurgles from his mouth and spews from his chest as he reaches for the phone, grasping at the cord.

He is able to pull the phone from its cradle. It hangs in front of him. But he is unable to reach the keypad.

                    TERENCE
        Hello?

                    OPERATOR (From phone)
                  (SOUNDS LIKE RECORDING)
If you would like to make a call,
please hang up, and try again.

Terence slumps over, his eyes rolling
dizzily into his head

TERENCE'S POV:

A blurred figure watches from a train cabin
as it leaves the station. Terence raises a
hand...tries to speak.

The phone booth, the departing train, the
platform, and even Terence's hand as he
waves it in front of his own face, fades to
BLACK.

BLACK SCREEN:

PHONE RINGING.

                    VOICE
Hello?

                    VOICE ON PHONE
               (Professional, MALE)
Hello? Geoffrey?

                    VOICE
               (Polite whisper)
Speaking.

                    VOICE ON PHONE
Hi, is this Mr. Geoffrey Oliver Davis?

                    VOICE
Yes. Who is this? Do I know you?

                    VOICE ON PHONE
You do now.

                    VOICE
What do you want?

FADE IN:

INT. GEOFFREY'S BEDROOM - NIGHT

GEOFFREY OLIVER DAVIS,(30s), handsome with
gaunt face, empty eyes, and hunched over
shoulders, lies in bed holding a phone to his
ear. An open magazine rests on his lap. On page
is a woman wearing a scanty bathing suit.

                    VOICE ON PHONE
To offer you the best deal of your life.
Tell me something Geoffrey...are you tired
of spending obscene amounts of money on car
insurance every
month?

                    GEOFF
You called me Geoffrey. You called me by my
first name like you were a friend of mine.

                    VOICE ON PHONE
I'm sorry. Would you prefer if I call you
Mr. Davis?

The room is dimly lit. A shade covers a
window that has no curtains. The walls are
bare.

                    GEOFF
Geoffrey is fine. What are you selling?
Insurance right?

Geoff turns the page in his magazine.

                    VOICE ON PHONE
Yes.

                    GEOFF
You called yesterday. We talked about my
parents...my job. You're Travis right?

                    VOICE ON PHONE
Yeah, that's right. I...think I remember
you.

                    GEOFF
When you called tonight, I thought you
remembered. But you're trying to sell me
insurance again. I told you you're welcome
to call if you want to talk to me. But you
also need to remove me from your call list.
I mean, don't get me wrong, I want to be
friends with you. But I don't need insurance
right now. You see, I don't have a car-

                    VOICE ON PHONE
Mr. Davis I have to go.

                    GEOFF
It was nice talking to you Travis.

DIAL TONE. Geoff hangs up. He turns the page
in the magazine.

INT. BRITTINGHAM PUBLISHING OFFICE - DAY

Geoffrey wheels a mail cart through a maze of office cubes while dropping letters and packages into little baskets.

The office is plain. The surroundings dismal. Bored office workers sip coffee in various cubes.

A closed off MAN in another ARGUES LOUDLY on the telephone. He turns, looks at Geoff as he slips a bouquet of mail into an empty box, then turns his back again, yelling profanely into the phone.

CARLA WHITE, an attractive twenty-six year old brunette sits in a cube, face buried in the pages of a manuscript. A screen saver flashes on her computer with the words "BEWARE OF DOG" scrolling by.

Geoff stops, stares at the back of her head.

                    CARLA
Just leave the mail in my basket and get lost.

Carla turns a page in the manuscript. HEAR THE PAGE TURNING LOUDLY, ECHOING IN the OFFICE...the SOUND RINGS HOLLOW WITH EMPTINESS.

                    GEOFF
Hear anything about Tarinskovsy's new book? Good stuff!

                    CARLA
Economic Reform in Post Cold war Russia and
the Mafia Who Controls it...
          (Yawn)
Yah...real page turner.

Carla rolls her eyes. Geoff leans against
the wall of her cubical comfortably.

                    GEOFF
I hear the murder rate per capita in Russia
is among the highest in Europe. In fact, it
rates as one of the highest in the world.
But I guess that wouldn't be of interest to
my favorite erotic thriller editor. How's
your latest edit coming?

                    CARLA
Great Geoff. Anything else?

                    GEOFF
Well, no...just uh, stopping by for a little
chat.

Carla sticks her tongue out of her mouth.
HEAR THE SOUND OF CARLA LICKING her thumb
before using it to turn another page of the
manuscript.

Geoff watches. Intently.

After a moment of uncomfortable silence,
Geoff slips out of Carla's cube and wheels
his cart down the aisle before stopping at
another cubicle. A sign over a mail basket
reads "LOUIS VOYENHEIMER".

Louis (40s), has the face of a man weathered with wrinkles from years of frowning. He wears slicked back hair, a pair of blue jeans, and a jacket with corduroy patches at the elbow.

A half eaten sandwich sits on his desk next to a coffee mug.

Geoff places mail in Louis' basket then moves to the next cube.

Louis stares after Geoff then leaves his desk. He grabs the mail as he follows Geoff.

                    LOUIS
DAVIS!

Geoff turns, finding himself face to face with a grim looking Louis.

                    GEOFF
Something wrong?

                    LOUIS
It's 1:30 and I'm just getting the mail. Is there a reason why I have to get mail this late? Do you have to start on the other side of the office every day? And what's with you putting the mail in the basket when I'm sitting right there? I'm right here, just put it in my hand.

                    GEOFF
Is that what you prefer?

                    LOUIS
I wouldn't be standing here if I was getting
what I preferred, now would I? I'd be at my
desk finishing my ham sandwich. A sandwich
my wife made before she left for work this
morning. A sandwich, I can hardly wait to
eat. But no, I'm standing here talking to
you about how you deliver the mail. Do I
sound like a happy man to you?

                    GEOFF
No. You sound like a prick.

Geoff wheels the cart away from Louis. After
landing a few pieces of mail into baskets
further down the aisle he stops by LIVIA
THORTON'S cubicle, shucking a bundle of mail
bound together by a single rubber band from
hand to hand like a football before tossing
it towards her desk.

LIVIA (Black, 32) turns around, catching the
bundle before it knocks over a cup of coffee.
African art and poetry line the walls of
Livia's cubical.

                    LIVIA
I saw your reflection on the computer
monitor.

Livia turns, batting eye lashes at Geoff.

                    GEOFF
I hear one of your authors made the bestsellers
list. Congratulations.

                         LIVIA
Thanks Geoff, though I can't take all of the
credit...I believe the writer had something to
do with it.

                         GEOFF
Don't sell yourself short. You were smart
enough to publish her book.

                         LIVIA
I know a good thing when I see it.

                         GEOFF
I haven't read it but I heard it's pretty
good. Capricorn Vern right?

                         LIVIA
I have an extra copy if you want to read it.

                         GEOFF
Sure. I'll stop by and pick it up tonight if
that's all right with you.

Livia smiles beautifully at Geoff, showing
pearly white teeth. Geoff pushes the cart
further down the aisle. Ahead, three
executive types block Geoff's path.

ROBERT BREAST, age twenty-five, good looking,
somewhat tall...JOHN CARTER, age thirty-two,
short with hulking shoulders, and GEORGE
ENGLEWOOD, thirty-five, slight build, and thick
glasses stand in the middle of the aisle in
Geoff's path.

                         JOHN
Geoff, my man...what's up? So, you porking
Livia Thorton or what?

George and Robert LAUGH, while looking over
their shoulders at an oblivious Livia, who
stands at her cubicle sifting through mail.

                    GEOFF
Actually, I prefer sex with women as opposed
to pigs. You might try it some time, but
then, you'd have to divorce your wife.

George, Robert, and John break into LAUGHTER.

                    ROBERT
Cut him some slack. We know who you really
like, right Geoff?

                    GEOFF
I have work to do.

Geoff tries pushing the cart through the
trio, but John stops the wheel with his
foot. WE HEAR THE WHEELS SQUEAKING TO A
HALT.

                    JOHN
I heard you asked Carla out for drinks and
she turned you down cold.

Geoff shoves the cart, rolling it over
John's foot.

INT. GEOFFREY'S BEDROOM - NIGHT

Geoff sits in bed, reading lamp over his
shoulder. He wears a tattered t-shirt, a
pair of sweat pants, and a pair of reading
glasses.

The caption on the book reads, *"How to Make Him Love Me"* by Capricorn Vern. The phone RINGS.

                    GEOFF
               (Into phone)
Hello?

                    FEMALE VOICE
               (From phone)
Mr. Davis? My name is Lydia and I'm calling on behalf of Tri-American Credit Card Company and you have been pre-approved for a credit card.

                    GEOFF
               (Smiling)
Hi Lydia.

Geoff takes his glasses off and closes the book.

                    FEMALE VOICE
               (From phone)
If I can just get some information from you we can get your card to you in six weeks.

                    GEOFF
Lydia, can I ask you something?

                    FEMALE VOICE
               (From phone)
Sure.

                    GEOFF
Are you married?

                    FEMALE VOICE
              (From phone, sounding thrown)
I'm sorry. I can only answer questions about
the credit card. I'm not allowed to answer
questions about my personal life, Mr. Davis.

                      GEOFF
So you think it's okay to call a complete
stranger and ask for personal information, but
it's not okay to give personal information
about yourself? Sounds a little one-sided to
me. I only give my personal information out to
my dear friends. I would like to be friends
with you, Lydia. Would that be possible?

                    FEMALE VOICE
                  (From phone)
I can get my supervisor for you-

                      GEOFF
No, that won't be necessary Lydia. I'm
ending this call, please take me off of your
call list.

Geoff hangs up, looks around the room. After
a few moments he grabs the phone and dials.

RINGING...

                RECORDED VOICE MESSAGE
                  (Automated Male)
Thank you for calling Line Reach telecom. To
reach customer service press one...To reach
our billing department press two...To
reach...

Geoff presses a button on the phone.

                    RECORDED VOICE MESSAGE
                      (Automated Female)
One moment connecting your call...

                    WOMAN'S VOICE (ON PHONE)
Thank you for calling Line Reach Telecom,
this is Tannie speaking, number you are
calling about please?

                            GEOFF
555-7771.

                    WOMAN'S VOICE (ON PHONE)
Am I speaking to Geoffrey Oliver Davis?

                            GEOFF
Yes.

                    WOMAN'S VOICE (ON PHONE)
How may I help you today, sir?

                            GEOFF
I would like to have my name and number
removed from the phone directory.

                    WOMAN'S VOICE (ON PHONE)
                       (Friendly)
Okay sir, that sounds like something I can
help you with. Would you like to have your
number unpublished or unlisted? There's a
difference. Unpublished means it won't be
listed in the phone book or with directory
assistance. Unlisted means it won't be
listed with directory assistance but can be
looked up in the phone book.

                            GEOFF
How about unpublished?

                    WOMAN'S VOICE (ON PHONE)
Great. We can remove you from directory
assistance right away. But it will be
another three weeks before your name is
removed from the phone book since it's
published once a year, usually in early
January.

                    GEOFF
That's fine.

                    WOMAN'S VOICE (ON PHONE)
Now, there is a five dollar a month charge
for this service.

                    GEOFF
Five dollars? I'm not spending five dollars
a month to keep telemarketers from trying to
get my money. Can I change the way I'm
listed in the phone book?

                    WOMAN'S VOICE (ON PHONE)
You can list your initials or your first
initial and last name or vice versa...

                    GEOFF
Okay. I'd like to be listed as G.O.D.

                    WOMAN'S VOICE ON PHONE
I'd love to help you sir, but I'm afraid you
can't be listed as a fictional character. It
has to be an actual person.

                    GEOFF
Fictional?

                    WOMAN'S VOICE ON PHONE
You can't list yourself as Barney Rubble or
Fred Flintstone...

                    GEOFF
No, I'm sorry you misunderstand. I'm using
my initials. G O D. Geoffrey Oliver Davis.

                    WOMAN'S VOICE (ON PHONE)
My apologies, I didn't realize...

                    GEOFF
No problem. Have you been working here long?

                    WOMAN'S VOICE (ON PHONE)
A few years.

                    GEOFF
Not bad...I've been with the company I work
with for about three years myself.

                    WOMAN'S VOICE (ON PHONE)
Is there anything else I can do for you Mr.
Davis?

                    GEOFF
No, I think that's it. So, are you married?

                    WOMAN'S VOICE (ON PHONE)
I'd love to talk with you Mr. Davis but I
have other customers trying to get through.
Thank you for calling Line Reach Telecom,
have a nice day.

Geoff hangs up. The light in his reading
lamp flickers, makes a buzzing noise,
flickers...then goes out.

INT. BRITTINGHAM PUBLISHING - DAY

We follow a line of cubicles to the end
where Geoff sits. His computer is off. A
mail cart is pushed against the wall.

Louis, looking disgruntled, finds Geoff and
delivers a manuscript, slamming it on his
desk without warning.

                    GEOFF
What's this?

                    LOUIS
A puppy.
          (Pause)
What does it look like you dolt? It's a
manuscript.

Geoff stares at the bundle.

                    LOUIS
It's not going to bite you. Take it. Read
it. Absorb it. Just don't let it get away.
And maybe someday you'll live down letting
"*50 Shades of Grey*" slip through our
fingers.

                    GEOFF
Obviously someone didn't think it was good
or they wouldn't be giving it to me.

                    LOUIS
Just be glad you're getting a second chance.
Try not to judge it based on the fact that
we put it in your grubby little paws.

Geoff stares at Louis.

                    GEOFF
Get someone else. I can't do this.

                    LOUIS
Tough shit kid. It's all yours.

Louis growls then walks away.

Geoff glares at the cover page.

                    GEOFF
                 (Mumbling)
Sam Houston..."*What Dreams Become*". Fucking
great. How in the hell am I supposed to
green light my own manuscript?

EXT. CITY STREET - NIGHT

Geoff pulls his coat closed. The wind stirs
and rattles trash inside a wire garbage can.
Helpless and cold he shivers, and races up
the empty city block.

EXT. CITY STREET - SAME

Livia Thorton, neck wrapped tightly in a scarf,
goes up the stairs of a brownstone apartment
building. She takes her keys out of her purse
and opens the door with shaky hands. Across the
street, a FIGURE IN BLACK lurks in the shadows.

INT. LIVIA'S LIVING ROOM - SAME

Livia walks in, closes the door, bolts three
heavy locks, then gives the door a firm
shake before throwing her purse on the
couch.

A door on the other side of the living room
opens. A CHILD, black, about six years-old
strolls in. The child's name is JOSH.

                    JOSH
Mommy!

They hug.

                    LIVIA
Hey sweetie. Where's Monica?

                    JOSH
Sleeping.

Livia smiles.

                    LIVIA
She's tired. We'll let her sleep in your
Bed tonight and we can sleep in mine.

                    JOSH
It's safer.

                    LIVIA
Yes, much safer.

Livia stares at Josh.

                    LIVIA
It's late. You go on to my room and let me
get settled. Okay?

                    JOSH
Okay!

Josh runs out of the room. Livia goes to the
window. She opens the curtains and peeks
out.

                    MONICA (OS)
I must have been really tired.

Livia turns, slightly startled.

                    MONICA
Sorry, I didn't mean to scare you.

MONICA 20s, white, with long hair and
attractive features stands across the room
with a physics text book in her arms. She
yawns loudly then flops on the couch.

                    LIVIA
Sleeping on the job?

                    MONICA
I was studying and dozed off. I got finals
tomorrow.

                    LIVIA
Why don't you sleep over? The school is only
ten minutes away from here. It doesn't make
sense to go all the way home only to come
back early in the morning.

                    MONICA
Cool. Thanks.

They smile.

                    MONICA
Well, I'm off to bed.

                    LIVIA
Good luck on your test tomorrow.

                    MONICA
Trust me, it's gonna take a lot more
than luck. More like a miracle.

Monica gets up, stretches, then leaves
the room. Livia goes into the kitchen.

INT. KITCHEN - SAME

Livia grabs a carton from the refrigerator
then moves to the counter where she pours a
glass of milk.

INT. LIVING ROOM - SAME

The top lock on the door turns as if someone
is using a key.

INT. KITCHEN - SAME

Livia pours milk into a glass. She gazes out
of the kitchen into the living room and
keeps pouring...the milk overflowing from
the glass onto the counter. There is fear in
her eyes. She stops pouring and grabs a
towel to stop the spillage.

INT. LIVING ROOM - SAME

The top bolt on the door makes a full turn
into an unlocked position. The doorknob
jiggles.

INT. KITCHEN - SAME

Livia grabs a butcher knife, then heads into
the living room.

INT. LIVING ROOM - SAME

The second lock on the door turns as if
someone is using a key. The doorknob
jiggles.

Livia raises the butcher knife over her head
and stares trance-like at the door.

                    MONICA (O.S.)
Livia! Are you okay?

Monica takes the knife from Livia.

                    LIVIA
Look...

Monica stares at the door.

                    MONICA
I don't see anything.

                    LIVIA
I locked those two bolts. And now they're
unlocked.

                    MONICA
It's after nine, you're tired and going a
little crazy.

                    LIVIA
I was standing right here and someone was
unlocking the door like they had a key.

                    MONICA
Are you sure you locked it?

                    LIVIA
The third bolt is still locked. Why would I
skip the first two and lock the third?

                    MONICA
Beats me. When I'm tired I don't know
whether I'm coming or going...why don't you
go to bed and I can keep an eye on Josh
while you get some rest.

                    LIVIA
No. I'm fine. You better get to sleep so you
can pass that exam tomorrow.

                    MONICA
Promise me you'll get some rest?

Livia nods.

INT. BRITTINGHAM PUBLISHING - DAY

Livia sits in her cubicle, cell phone
pressed against her ear.

                    LIVIA
               (Into phone)
I need someone at my apartment at
6 o'clock.
               (Beat)
I'm not waiting till nine, damn it! Yes, I
know there are other people ahead of me
but...(SIGH) Okay. Thank you.

Livia hangs up.

                    LIVIA
Unbelievable!

Geoff wheels his cart by Livia's cubicle and drops mail into her basket. Livia turns to look at Geoff.

                    LIVIA
Are you busy tonight?

                    GEOFF
What did you have in mind?

                    LIVIA
I need the locks on my door changed.

                    GEOFF
Sure. I can help. If that's what you need.

                    LIVIA
Stop by my place after work? I'll call and order the locks and pick them up on the way.

                    GEOFF
What about Josh? Aren't you picking him up from basketball practice today?

                    LIVIA
Yeah. You're right. Damn it. Wait a minute… how'd you know that?

                    GEOFF
I guess you mentioned it before. I can pick the keys up on the way if you want.

                    LIVIA
Would you?

                    GEOFF
Of course. Anything for you and my favorite little buddy.

INT. LIVIA'S APARTMENT/LIVING ROOM - NIGHT

Livia stands behind Geoff who kneels as he drills a screw into the panel of her door.

                    GEOFF
Looks like I got everything installed.

                    LIVIA
Thanks Geoff, I really appreciate your help. I've been a nervous wreck.

                    GEOFF
No problem.

Geoff goes into his pocket and pulls out a little plastic bag. He holds it so Livia sees.

                    GEOFF
Fuck.

                    LIVIA
What?

                    GEOFF
You might have to take this back. Looks like you've been screwed out of a key.

Livia examines the bag.

                    LIVIA
You can't take it back, we already installed it.

Geoff searches his tool bag for the extra key.

                    GEOFF
There's usually two sets of keys.

                    LIVIA
Don't worry about it. I'll have another one
made.

Livia takes the plastic bag. Geoff shrugs.

                    GEOFF
Sure. Whatever floats your boat.

                    LIVIA
So…what do I owe you for this? 50 bucks?
A drink?

                    GEOFF
Put it on my tab.

                    LIVIA
Josh will be here with Monica in a few
minutes. I was hoping the two of you could
meet?

                    GEOFF
Some other time. I gotta run.

Geoff leans in and gives Livia a friendly
kiss on the cheek. She moves away, slightly
taken aback by the gesture. They laugh.

                    LIVIA
You're such a goofball.

                    GEOFF
See you Monday.

Geoff walks out. Livia closes the door.

EXT. CITY STREET - NIGHT

Geoff drags a sparse 4 ft. tall Christmas tree through dirty city snow. The city is grim, dark. Bundled up pedestrians move hastily in opposite directions on a lonely city street.

INT. GEOFFREY'S LIVING ROOM - LATER

Geoff decorates the tiny Christmas tree with tinsel and ornaments.

Tree garland hangs over the window and an electric singing Santa sits on the table rolling his hips as it plays the ukulele.

Geoff flops down on top of a leather sofa. A dusty old window shade shields him from the outside world. An old fashioned typewriter sits unused in the corner.

Lights from Geoff's television flickers on the wall.

"Miracle on 34th Street" plays on screen.

INT. LIVIA'S LIVING ROOM - NIGHT

Josh and Livia sit snug on the couch. The window curtains are pulled back. Fireworks are on display in the sky.

                    JOSH
Happy New Year Mommy!

                    LIVIA
Happy New Year, baby. Can we go to sleep now?

                    JOSH
But it's only midnight.

Livia tickles Josh who explodes with
laughter.

                   LIVIA
Only midnight? Kids all over the world are
asleep right now. You're going to bed.

                    JOSH
But it's New Year's and if I go to sleep
you'll think about daddy and cry.

Livia gets up, turns away from Josh.

                    JOSH
I'm sorry. I didn't mean to make you sad.

                   LIVIA
You didn't make me sad.

                    JOSH
I'm sorry.

                   LIVIA
Stop apologizing. You didn't do anything
wrong, okay? And I'm not lonely or sad...
as long as I have you

Livia and Josh hug.

                    JOSH
Can we watch the fireworks a little longer?

                   LIVIA
Sure...but only for a few minutes. Josh
leans over the back of the couch to watch
the fireworks.

Livia stares at a picture resting on top of the fireplace. The MAN in the picture is TERENCE THORTON.

                    JOSH
Mama? Who is that?

Livia looks out of the window.

A SHADOW fades into the darkness of a nearby alley, eyes watching them from across the street. Livia leaps off of the couch and pulls the curtains closed.

Josh stares at his mother, stunned.

                    LIVIA
We're going to bed.

                    JOSH
But I thought...

                    LIVIA
              (Firmly)
I said we're going to bed.

Livia grabs Josh and pulls him away from the window.

INT. GEOFFREY'S BATHROOM - NIGHT

Geoff showers. The phone RINGS.

He pulls the shower curtains back, grabs a towel, then skips out of the bathroom.

INT. GEOFFREY'S BEDROOM - NIGHT

Geoff answers the ringing phone.

                    GEOFF
Hello?

                    GIRL'S VOICE
Hello?

                    GEOFF
Can I help you?

                    GIRL'S VOICE
God...?

                    GEOFF
Excuse me?

                    GIRL'S VOICE
I'm asking. Are you really God?

Geoff sits on the edge of the bed.

                    GEOFF
I'm whoever you want me to be. What makes
you think I'm God?

                    GIRL'S VOICE
You have to be! I just know you are. I
prayed and I prayed for a sign and there you
were, right there in the phone book. Cindy.
Don't you know me?

Geoff leans forward, intrigued.

                    GEOFF
               (After a pause)
What can I do for you Cindy?

                  GIRL'S VOICE
I'm pregnant.
          (Sobbing)
And I don't know how to tell my mom and dad.

                    GEOFF
How did you get my number?

                  GIRL'S VOICE
My dad is going to kill me.
          (Sob)
He is literally going to kill me.

Geoff sits in stunned silence.

                  GIRL'S VOICE
Hello? Are you still there?

                    GEOFF
Yeah...I'm here. Can you talk to your mom?

                  GIRL'S VOICE
I think so.

                    GEOFF
She'll be disappointed. But she'll help you.
Tell your mom, Cindy.

                  GIRL'S VOICE
          (Sob)
I'm so scared...

                    GEOFF
Talk to your parents. Will you do that for
me? Will you do that for yourself?

                    GIRL'S VOICE
I...I was hoping I could not be pregnant
anymore.

                    GEOFF
It doesn't work that way, Cindy. You have
to understand...things happen for a reason.
Talk to your parents. They'll help you.

                    GIRL'S VOICE
I'll try.

                    GEOFF
Good. I have to go now. I hope it works out
for you.

                    GIRL'S VOICE
Can I call you again?

                    GEOFF
Anytime, Cindy.

Geoff hangs up. He lays back on the bed,
towel still wrapped around his dampened body
as he stares at the ceiling.

INT. LIVIA'S BEDROOM - SAME

Livia lies in bed. The phone RINGS. She
answers, holding the phone to her ear.

                    LIVIA
Hello?

Livia holds the phone, quietly listening.
The sound of a MAN GROANING filters into her
earpiece.

Livia slowly hangs up.

INT. GEOFF'S BEDROOM - SAME

Geoff holds the phone to his ear. A LOUD
CLICKING NOISE FILTERS THROUGH THE RECEIVER,
FOLLOWED BY A DIAL TONE.

Geoff hangs up.

INT. GEOFFREY'S BEDROOM - NIGHT

Geoff sleeps. The room is dark but a light
beaming from an open bathroom door shines
down on him. THE PHONE RINGS.

Geoff answers.

                    GEOFF
Hello?

                    STRANGER (on phone)
Are you really him?

                    GEOFF
Depends on who you're talking about.

                    STRANGER (on phone)
Does omniscient Ever-Powerful Spirit ring a
bell?

                    GEOFF
It's 3 a.m. Call me at a decent hour and
we'll talk.

                    STRANGER (on phone)
                (Menacing whisper)
You're supposed to be there when we need you
but again, you never are.

Geoff sits up.

                    GEOFF
Who is this?

                    STRANGER (on phone)
You see all. You're supposed to
be everywhere, in everything...and yet,
you don't know who I am.

                    GEOFF
I'd love to have a philosophical chat with
you, but some other time.

                    STRANGER (on phone)
But I need to talk right now.

                    GEOFF
Call me in the morning. Whatever it is can
wait.
          (Firmly)
Now goodbye.

                    STRANGER (on phone)
Don't hang up on me. I'm warning you.

Geoff slams the phone down.

A second passes. The phone RINGS again.
Geoff slinks into the cushions of his bed
and goes back to sleep.

INT. BRITTINGHAM PUBLISHING - DAY

Geoff wheels his mail cart down the aisle.
He stops at Livia's cubicle. She has just
entered her work station, settling in.

Livia throws her purse and set of keys on
the desk. Geoff lays the book nearby.

                    LIVIA
Well, hello stranger. Long time no see.

                    GEOFF
I've been around. Keeping busy?

                    LIVIA
Pretty much. Got a lot on my mind this week.

                    GEOFF
Anything I can help you with?

Livia sighs. She looks depressed.

                    LIVIA
Not really.

Geoff kneels next tc Livia's chair and
fishes through the contents of his mail
basket.

                    GEOFF
How's Josh?

                    LIVIA
He's okay.

A picture of Terence Thorton sits on Livia's
desk. She gazes longincly at his picture.

                    GEOFF
How is he handling...?

                    LIVIA
He's hanging in there.

                    GEOFF
I'm sorry for everything that happened.

                    LIVIA
What for? It's not like you killed
him.

Geoff eyes the picture of Terence.

                    GEOFF
Listen...you have my phone number. Give me
a call if you need anything.

                    LIVIA
Be careful. I might take you up on that.

John, George, and Robert walk by. Robert
rolls a sheet of paper into a ball and
shoots it into Livia's wastebasket.

                    ROBERT
Three pointer!

John makes a sexual gesture then nods at
Livia who is facing her computer, completely
oblivious of the exchange.

Geoff gives him the finger.

Livia packs her briefcase then turns her
computer off.

                    GEOFF
So where are you off to?

                    LIVIA
Carla and I are about to grab a cup of
coffee. You coming with us?

                    GEOFF
I'm busy. But do me a favor and tell Carla I
love her.

                    LIVIA
Tell her yourself, you goof ball. I have to
go.

                    GEOFF
Peace out.

Livia rolls her eyes and scoots by.

Geoff leans coolly against the cubical wall
which gives way, nearly collapsing to the
floor.

Livia stifles a giggle as Geoff puts the
cubicle wall back in place.

INT. CAFÉ - LATER

Livia and Carla sit on opposite ends of the
table. Carla sits with her legs folded
beneath her.

                    CARLA
I don't know what to do. He hasn't proposed.
It's been two fucking years.

                    LIVIA
Let him go. There's plenty of fish in the
sea...and by the way, there's a fish swimming
around the office and he's got his eyes on
you.

                    CARLA
Oh God. Not him. Anybody but that loser.

                    LIVIA
He's a nice guy once you get to know him.
Don't do him like that. He's such a cutie.

                    CARLA
If he's so cute then why don't you date him?

                    LIVIA
There's only one man for me and he's not
here anymore.

Carla stretches across the table, resting
one of her hands on top of Livia's.

                    CARLA
I'm sorry. It's still too soon.

                    LIVIA
You never really get over it. I don't care
what people say. I look at Josh and think
about his father every single day.

Carla sighs.

                    CARLA
You're right. Besides… it wouldn't work out
with Geoff anyway. He's too much of an
idiot.

INT.BRITTINGHAM PUBLISHING/FLASHBACK - NIGHT

Geoff walks into Carla's dimly lit cubicle
with two cups of coffee. Carla closes a
manuscript and walks toward Geoff.

He fumbles with the coffee cup mugs
anxiously as she nears him.

                    GEOFF
It's hot.

Geoff offers the coffee to Carla but she ignores
it.

                    CARLA
So are you.

Carla moves in for a kiss but Geoff
accidently spills the scolding hot coffee
down the front of her blouse.

                    CARLA
          Wailing)
SHIT.

                    GEOFF
Oh fuck! Sorry...

Geoff fans the spill but accidently smacks
Carla across the breasts, injuring her even
more.

                    CARLA
You moron...you fucking burned my tits!
Don't touch me.

Geoff steps out of Carla's cubicle.

                    GEOFF
I'll get some towels.

                    CARLA
Don't get anything--just leave.

INT. COFFEE SHOP - CONTINUE

PRESENT DAY

                    CARLA
Geoff is obsessed with me. I think it's
creepy.

                    LIVIA
He's lonely.

There is a look of sadness in Livia's eyes.

                    CARLA
Why are you even friends with that loser?
Seriously?

                    LIVIA
Terence and Geoff were best friends. I miss
my husband too much. I'm so lonely.
Sometimes I want to surround myself with the
people he was closest to.

Tense silence.

                    CARLA
I'm sorry. I don't know what to say. I just
want you to feel happy again. I miss *you*.

Carla drains the rest of her coffee.

                    LIVIA
I'm trying.

                    CARLA
I know, hun. Let's do this again. Okay?

INT. GEOFFREY'S LIVING ROOM - NIGHT

Geoff sits in front of an old fashioned typewriter and stares at a blank white page.

INT. CAFE/FLASHBACK - NIGHT

Geoff and Livia sit in an empty café, drinking coffee. Waiters collect dishes nearby. An old man reads the paper a few tables away.

Livia takes a sip of coffee.

                    LIVIA
What happened to that book you wrote?

Geoff sighs.

                    GEOFF
Rejected by the publisher… so I'm starting over.

                    LIVIA
I'm more than happy to read it if you want.

                    GEOFF
Really?

                    LIVIA
Why not?

Geoff gazes lovingly at Livia. She takes another sip of coffee then waves a hand in front of his face.

                    LIVIA
Earth to Geoff!

Geoff shakes his head, embarrassed.

                    GEOFF
Sorry I'm..

                    LIVIA
You okay?

                    GEOFF
Yeah...I'm fine...

                    LIVIA
Then why are you looking at me like that?

He grabs her hand.

                    GEOFF
I can't take my eyes off of you. I love you,
Livia. I've always loved you.

He waits for a reaction. Livia looks
surprised by the revelation at first, then
embarrassed. Geoff leaps across the table
and tries to kiss Livia. She shrinks away.

                    LIVIA
Don't-

She puts a hand up. Crushed, Geoff sits down
again, takes a sip of his coffee.

                    LIVIA
I-I have to go. Terence and I are going to
dinner.

Livia hastily gathers her coat and shopping
bag and scurries away.

EXT. BROWNSTONE (PRESENT DAY)- NIGHT

Monica leaves the brownstone and walks down
the stairs. A cold breeze whips her hair and
stiff wool coat into a frenzy. She pulls it
closed and digs her face into the collar of
her coat to shield herself from the biting
wind.

Geoff steps out of the darkness and stands
in front of the brownstone before Monica.

Monica stares icily at him until a look of
recognition crosses her face.

                    MONICA
Do I know you from somewhere?

                    GEOFF
I don't think so. I'm here to see Livia.
We work together.

Monica looks at her watch.

                    MONICA
At this time of night?

                    GEOFF
Is she busy?

                    MONICA
She's asleep. That busy enough for you?

                    GEOFF
I guess I'll catch her at work.

                    MONICA
Really? Ah. I see...

Catching Monica's hint, Geoff shifts, embarrassed.

                    GEOFF
It's not like that. I swear.

                    MONICA
Yeah, right!

                    GEOFF
C'mon. Do I look like the kind of man who would lie to a pretty lady like you?

                    MONICA
You look like a guy who's after something.

Monica shucks side to side, keeping warm.

                    GEOFF
Are you married?

                    MONICA
Do I look married?

                    GEOFF
You look like you should be…

Monica smiles.

                    GEOFF
There's a diner down the street.
Care for a cup of coffee?

                    MONICA
Sorry, I gotta catch the A-train. It's the last one running.

                    GEOFF
The subway? This time of night?

                    MONICA
I carry a can of pepper spray.

                    GEOFF
     Nice...

Geoff and Monica leave the brownstone
together.

The stranger watches from across the street.

INT. GEOFFREY'S LIVING ROOM - NIGHT

Geoff paces the room with the phone to his
ear.

                    GEOFF
Hello Carrie, what can I do for you?

                    CARRIE (ON PHONE)
My boyfriend is leaving me.

                    GEOFF
Why? What did you do?

                    CARRIE (ON PHONE)
What do you mean? I didn't do anything.

                    GEOFF
Maybe that's the problem, Carrie.

Geoff hangs up.

INT. GEOFFREY'S LIVING ROOM - LATER

Geoff continues to pace, appearing almost
professional as he presses the phone to his
ear.

                    GEOFF
Who is this?

                    BILL (ON PHONE)
BILL.

                    GEOFF
What do you want Bill? I'm god. I'm busy.
You're not the only person in the world with
problems. I got problems too. My problem is
trying to solve your problems.

                    BILL (ON PHONE)
I'm sorry I just-

                    GEOFF
Come on, spit it out. I don't have all
night.

                    BILL (ON PHONE)
My wife doesn't appreciate me. The kids hate
me. I work all day, I pay all the bills. I
give them everything they want.

                    GEOFF
What do you want me to do?

                    BILL (ON PHONE)
How do I get them to respect me?

                    GEOFF
Leave. Don't pack your bags. Just put your
shoes on and walk out. When your wife is
crying about the house and the kids are
whining about not having cool clothes and
bikes, and all that other bullshit they want
that you pay for, let's see how much respect
they have for dear ole dad.

                    BILL (ON PHONE)
I can't do that.

                    GEOFF
Find yourself a good fuck and move on. Be a
man.

Geoff hangs up. The phone RINGS.

                    GEOFF
For fuck's sake.

Second ring, Geoff answers, sitting down.

                    STRANGER (ON PHONE)
Hello?

                    GEOFF
I'm a busy man, what do you want?

                    STRANGER (ON PHONE)
You can start by answering my question.

                    GEOFF
Okay...let's hear it.

                    STRANGER (ON PHONE)
Why am I here?

                    GEOFF
Why do you think? We are all here to do the
same thing. Live for a short time and die.
End of discussion.

                    STRANGER (ON PHONE)
Why?

                    GEOFF
It's the cruel reality of our existence.
You're a cockroach on the asshole of time.
Life is misery. Get over it.

                    STRANGER (ON PHONE)
Then what's the point of living?

                    GEOFF
There is no point to living. The journey is
figuring that out. You live and you die, and
that's it. You decide whether your life is
meaningful or not.

                    STRANGER (ON PHONE)
But you said, there's no point.

                    GEOFF
I know what I said.

                    STRANGER (ON PHONE)
We live such complicated lives. And in the
end, we die?

                    GEOFF
That's life.

                    STRANGER (ON PHONE)
No. It's death. The only thing we are all
guaranteed in this life.

                    GEOFF
If you want to look at it that way.

                    STRANGER (ON PHONE)
Man builds the world in his own image. He
has the power to choose, but no power to
escape the necessity of choice.

                    GEOFF
Ayn Rand?

                    STRANGER
You're a literary man. You tell me.

                    GEOFF
Who are you?

                    STRANGER
I'm the one pulling the strings.

                    GEOFF
Is that right, dick head?

                    STRANGER
You should know. You're God.

                    GEOFF
I think I've had enough of this...

                    STRANGER
But you didn't help me.

                    GEOFF
You were busy. Babbling.

                    STRANGER
I'm a bit overwhelmed at the moment. That's
why I'm calling you.

                    GEOFF
I'm saving the world one soul at a time and
YOU'RE overwhelmed?

                    STRANGER (ON PHONE)
I killed someone tonight.

Geoff sits back, stunned.

                    GEOFF
Why?

                    STRANGER (ON PHONE)
I killed her because she was useless.

                    GEOFF
Who the fuck do you think you are? You don't
get to decide who lives or who dies. You're
not God.

                    STRANGER (ON PHONE)
Neither are you.

Geoff falls silent, frowning.

                    STRANGER (ON PHONE)
Then again, we're all gods...in our way. We
create life when we make love. We end life,
when we murder.

                    GEOFF
Did you really kill someone?

The stranger LAUGHS.

                    STRANGER (ON PHONE)
You're god. You tell me.

                    GEOFF
I don't know if you did or didn't.

                    STRANGER(ON PHONE)
Then you're not really God are you?

                    GEOFF
I'm whoever you want me to be.

                    STRANGER (ON PHONE)
You're the puppeteer. I know all about you.

                    GEOFF
Good. Then you know I'm about to hang up.

                    STRANGER (ON PHONE)
I told you before...don't hang up on me.

Geoff hangs up.

INT. GEOFFREY'S BEDROOM - LATER

The phone RINGS and RINGS. Geoff jumps out
of bed and rips the phone cord from out of
the wall.

                    GEOFF
Jeez...will you back off already?!

Geoff pulls the covers over his head.

INT. GEOFF'S BEDROOM - MORNING

The thin shade that usually covers the
window is pulled to the top. Blinding
sunlight streams into the room, directly

onto the phone, which is thrown across the floor.

Geoff grabs it and checks the cord for damage. After plugging it into the wall he sits the phone on the night stand.

Right away, the phone begins to ring. Geoff ignores it. He sits on the edge of the bed, eyes baggy from lack of rest as he slides a pair of socks onto his feet.

He stands, zips his pants, buttons his shirt, then grabs a tie and wraps it around his neck.

The phone RINGS again. Finally, he answers.

                    GEOFF
               (Into phone)
Hello?

A woman's scream filters through the receiver.

Geoff pulls the phone away from his ear.

The scream is followed by a gurgling sound, succeeded by tense quiet. With trembling fingers Geoff slowly and curiously brings the receiver close to his face.

                    STRANGER (ON PHONE)
See what you made me do?

Geoff pulls the phone over to the window and closes the shade.

                    GEOFF
Who the fuck is this?

                    STRANGER (ON PHONE)
You're god. You tell me who I am.

                    GEOFF
If this is one of the guys pulling a prank-
Listen, I want nothing to do with this.

                    STRANGER (ON PHONE)
Boo hoo.

                    GEOFF
What did you do?

                    STRANGER (ON PHONE)
I did exactly what you wanted.

                    GEOFF
I'm calling the cops.

                    STRANGER (ON PHONE)
And what will they do? Trace the line to a
phone booth somewhere in the middle of the
city? You're a bigger joke than I thought.

                    GEOFF
Who do you think I'm...look man, it was just
a joke. You don't really think I'm...

                    STRANGER (ON PHONE)
Oh but I do...only weaker and more pathetic
than I envisioned.

                    GEOFF
I don't know who you think I am, but I'm not
God.

                    STRANGER (ON PHONE)
You're exactly right. And now you're gonna
pay until you answer my question.

                    GEOFF
What question?

                    STRANGER (ON PHONE)
Why?

DIAL TONE.

Panicked, Geoff dials a phone number. FOUR
LONG RINGS filters through the receiver.

                    LIVIA (ON PHONE)
Hello?

Geoff hangs up, relieved.

INT. BRITTINGHAM PUBLISHING - DAY

Geoff wheels his mail cart down the aisle.
He sweats profusely. A huge circle of sweat
stains the underarms of his crisp white
shirt.

Geoff stops at Livia's cubicle. She turns to
look at Geoff.

                    LIVIA
Are you okay? You look sick.

Geoff nods, wheeling his cart away from her
mailbox. Livia follows.

                    LIVIA
Seriously...are you okay?

                    GEOFF
I'm a sick man. Just not in the way you
think.

Geoff waits until Livia is close. She lays
an open palm on his forehead.

                    LIVIA
Oh my god, you're burning up. You should go
home.

                    GEOFF
There's no heat in my apartment.

                    LIVIA
Well, no wonder. Of course you're gonna get
sick living in an unheated apartment this
time of year. What happened?

                    GEOFF
The radiator stopped working. The janitor
can't seem to fix it.

                    LIVIA
You stay at my place until it's up and
running. Josh and I can make you soup.

                    GEOFF
I can rent a room at the YMCA or stay at a
hotel.

                    LIVIA
Whatever. I'll see you tonight.

The phone RINGS.

Livia goes to her cubicle and answers the phone. Moments pass. Geoff is on standby, watching fidgeting as Livia returns.

                    LIVIA
Josh is at home alone. Monica never showed up. We can leave together if you want.

                    GEOFF
I don't want to intrude….

The look on Geoff's face says the opposite.

                    LIVIA
Stop it! You're sleeping over whether
you want to or not… poor thing.

Livia gathers her purse and other personal effects, links her arm into Geoff's, and drags him out of the office.

                    LIVIA
When you're better and back in your apartment, you can get a couple of space heaters.

INT. SUBWAY - DAY

A tall man, 30s, average looks, with a muscular build studies a grisly crime scene near a phone booth in the subway. He is detective NEAL HARRISON.

His partner (Asian, 40s), stands by his side. He is DETECTIVE LEE.

A crowd of police officers and investigators surround a single phone booth. The area has

been sealed off by police tape. Officers
scurry about.

Neal and Lee flash their badges at officers
as they near the victim's body. Detective
Neal pulls the white sheet covering the
victim away from her face.

                    NEAL
This looks eerily familiar.

                    LEE
I've seen this before. This scene.

A young uniformed OFFICER appears behind the
detectives, standing over their shoulders.

                    OFFICER
Sir, we found a wallet nearby.

Neal takes the wallet and examines it.

                    NEAL
We investigated a murder in this booth two
years ago.

                    LEE
The shooting victim. You thinkin' what
I'm thinkin'?

                    NEAL
It's a long shot.

                    LEE
Let's notify next of kin and look over some
contacts from the earlier case.

                    NEAL
Why?

                    LEE
Call it a hunch.

                    NEAL
You always got a hunch. Put an L on it and
make it lunch and we're in business.

                    LEE
Hasn't let me down yet.

                    NEAL
What, lunch?

                    LEE
No. *Man*, get something to eat, please.

INT. LIVIA'S LIVING ROOM - DAY

Livia, followed by Geoff, walks in.

                    LIVIA
Have a seat Geoff. Make yourself at home and
I'll make some tea.

Livia goes into the kitchen. Geoff sits. He
looks up to find Josh standing at the door
watching him.

                    GEOFF
Hello.

Josh takes a step in a direction opposite
of Geoff then eyes him suspiciously.

                         JOSH
I've seen you before. At my school.

Geoff and Josh stare each other down. Livia
returns with a cup of tea in her hand.

                         GEOFF
Thank you.

                         LIVIA
No problem. I'll get Josh's room ready for
you.

                         GEOFF
No way. I'll take the couch.

                         LIVIA
He sleeps in my bed most nights anyway so we
might as well put the room to use.

INT. LIVIA'S BEDROOM - NIGHT

Livia and Josh lay in bed. Livia closes the
storybook in her hand and turns the light
off. She wraps her arms around Josh.

                         LIVIA
You're quiet.

                         JOSH
I saw him before, Mommy. At my school.

                         LIVIA
Of course you've seen him before. Remember
he played softball with your dad at the
park? That's probably where you remember
him from.

                    JOSH
Okay.

                    LIVIA
You believe me?

Josh nods.

                    LIVIA
Good. I feel safe. Don't you? I trust Geoff.
What about you?

Josh closes his eyes.

INT. LIVIA'S HALLWAY - SAME

Geoff listens on the other side of Livia's
bedroom door.

                    GEOFF
You're a very lucky man, Josh.

 INT. LIVIA'S LIVING ROOM - MORNING

Livia is fully dressed and carrying her
briefcase. Geoff is in sweats resting on the
couch. Josh joins Livia at the door. He's
fully dressed in a school uniform and wears
his backpack.

                    LIVIA
Geoff, there's food in the cupboards and in
the fridge if you get hungry. You'll find
the appliances are easy to use, so there
should be no problem there.

                    GEOFF
I can pick Josh up from school.

                    LIVIA
No, I'll wait for Monica. Besides, you're
sick. You might as well milk all the rest
you can get out of this deal. I can call
your landlord and see if he's gotten
things fixed?

Livia opens the door. Detectives Henry Lee
and Neal Harrison stand on the other side.
Livia recoils, surprised.

                    NEAL
Hi. You Livia Thorton?

                    LIVIA
Yes.

                    NEAL
I'm detective Harrison, and this is my
partner Detective Henry Lee.

                    LEE
You mind if we come in and talk?

                    LIVIA
If I can see your badges?

                    NEAL
Sure.

The men open their wallets and quickly flash
their badges. Livia moves to the side,
allowing the men to walk in. The officers
look around.

                    LIVIA
Can I help you?

                    LEE
Monica Sing? You know her?

                    LIVIA
Yes. Is something wrong?

The officers look at each other then back at
Livia.

                    NEAL
When was the last time you saw her?

                    LIVIA
Two nights ago? Why?

                    LEE
Was she alive?

                    LIVIA
Of course she was alive. Will you tell me
what the hell is going on?? What do you mean
'was she alive'?

                    NEAL
Ms. Sing was murdered.

Josh wraps his arms around Livia's waist.

                    LIVIA
Geoff, will you take care of Josh?

Geoff leaves the sofa and tenderly pulls
Josh away from Livia. She tries to regroup
but her face wrought with grief.

                    GEOFF
I'll go with him.

Josh and Geoff leave. Officer Lee stares
after them.

                    LEE
So she was alive when you saw her last?

Livia folds her arms.

                    LIVIA
I just told you she was a minute ago.

                    NEAL
What was the extent of your relationship
with Miss Sing?

                    LIVIA
She was a good friend and Josh's babysitter.
How did she die?

                    LEE
We can't divulge any of the details at this
time but we can tell you we found her not
too far from where you live. Did she often
travel late hours to and from your home?

Livia takes a deep breath. Neal offers an
unsympathetic grin.

                    LIVIA
Sometimes… or she would spend the night.

                    NEAL
Where were you about one a.m. the night
before last?

                    LIVIA
I was here with Josh.

Lee opens a notepad then reads from the
page.

                    LEE
              (After a pause)
Were you with Josh two years ago when your
husband was murdered?

                    LIVIA
Excuse me?

                    NEAL
Your husband. He was murdered about two
years ago. Correct?

                    LIVIA
Wait a minute...what in the hell is this?
Are you accusing me of something?

                    NEAL
We're just finding it a bit coincidental...
if you will, that your husband was shot
and killed in a subway two years ago. And
now your babysitter meets a similar fate at
the same location. Which also happens to be
in close proximity to your home.

Josh's bedroom door opens. Geoff comes out
and stands by Livia's side.

                    LIVIA
Why would I kill Monica? You're not making
sense.

                    LEE
Suppose your husband was having an affair
and you find out the woman he was having an
affair with was the babysitter?

                    LIVIA
Bullshit.   There's   no   relationship   or
connection to my husband's death.   I hired
Monica a year after my husband died.

                    NEAL
We'll look into it. Your husband's murder
is still unsolved. Maybe his killer will
lead us to Monica's murderer.

                    LIVIA
My husband was murdered two years ago and
now you want to find his killer?

                    GEOFF
Maybe you guys should leave and give us time
to absorb this tragedy. This is a bit of a
shock and Josh doesn't seem to be taking the
news well.

                    NEAL
Who the fuck are you?

                    GEOFF
I'm Livia's friend and co-worker.

Livia's lips begin to quiver as grief
visibly sets in.

                    LIVIA
We're done here. Get out.

Neal smiles, tucks his badge into his front
pocket then follows Detective Lee out the
front door.

                    NEAL
Don't worry. We'll see you again.

                    LIVIA
Don't count on it.

She slams the door shut behind them.

                    LIVIA
Who would do something like this?

Sobbing, Livia shrinks in despair as Geoff
wraps   an   arm   around   her   shoulders
consolingly.

                    GEOFF
I don't know what to say.

                    LIVIA
Why would they think I have something to do
with this?

                    GEOFF
Do   you   know   if   she   had   any   enemies?   A
boyfriend, maybe?

Livia sits down, covers her mouth with an
open hand.

                    GEOFF
What's wrong?

                    LIVIA
They're right. It's my fault. First Terence.
Now Monica. Someone did this because of me.

                    GEOFF
It's not your fault.

                    LIVIA
I just pray whoever it is won't try to hurt
Josh.

                    GEOFF
For what it's worth, I don't think you or
Josh are in danger.

                    LIVIA
Why?

                    GEOFF
The subway is dangerous. Especially
at night. What happened to Monica and
Terence was just a coincidence.

                    LIVIA
Tell that to the detectives. Or better yet,
tell it to whoever is watching me and Josh
night after night.

INT. DETECTIVE NEAL'S CAR - NIGHT

Lee slides into the passenger seat and
closes the door.

                    LEE
You rattled her pretty good. What do you
think?

                    NEAL
I don't think it's her.

                    LEE
Me either. What about the guy?

                    NEAL
What guy?

                    LEE
The one with her kid.

Neal and Lee look at each other.

                    NEAL
There was something off about him for
sure, but....

                    LEE
Is he her boyfriend? Did he know the victim
or even the husband? He seemed a little *too*
interested. I saw his shadow by the door. He
was listening.

                    NEAL
What's his motive? He said he was just a co-
worker.

                    LEE
I don't know. Get close to her?

                    NEAL
But why would he kill the babysitter?
Doesn't make sense.

                    LEE
Maybe she knew something about him.

                    NEAL
Two years later? I doubt it.

INT. GEOFFREY'S LIVING ROOM - NIGHT

Geoff enters, strips out of his clothes down
to a white t-shirt and a pair of boxers,
then throws his pants on the sofa.

                    GEOFF
And so it begins...

Racing to an old fashioned typewriter in the
corner of the room, Geoff slides into a

chair, inserts a sheet of paper into the old fashioned typewriter and begins to type.

HIGH ANGLE on Geoff typing furiously. We stay on Geoff with a shot of the window in the background. A figure watches from the sidewalk then slowly drifts into the darkness.

LATER

Geoff blows sweat from his brow, rips the sheet of paper from the typewriter, and marvels at his work.

The phone RINGS. Geoff sits the page on a nearby table then answers the phone.

                    GEOFF
Hello?

INT. STRANGER'S APARTMENT - SAME

The Stranger sits in front of a huge cross, which decorates his living room wall. The sofa he sits on is a dark red color. He wears a wife beater t-shirt, pants, and sweats profusely.

His face is obscured by darkness. An open bible sits before a lit candle.

                    STRANGER (into phone)
Are you ready to answer to my question?

INTERCUT: GEOFFREY'S LIVING ROOM / STRANGER'S
APARTMENT

Geoff clings to the phone.

                    GEOFF
What question?

The stranger throws the small statue of an
angel across the room in frustration then
bangs the phone on the couch.

                    STRANGER
WHY?

                    GEOFF
Why-and what are you doing?

The stranger turns to the cross on the wall.

                    STRANGER
I'm reading the bible. But you should
already know that.

                    GEOFF
I told you before, I'm not God.

                    STRANGER
I came to you for answers but all I get are
more questions.

                    GEOFF
I take it the answer in your bible aren't
good enough?

STRANGER
The bible says a lot of things. Doesn't mean all of it is true. Why I should remain a faithful servant when He failed me over and over again? My life is the culmination failure after failure. Other people are happy with their pathetic lot in life. It's unfair. Why me? Why not me?

Geoff sighs.

GEOFF
I don't know. I-I can't answer that. It's random.

STRANGER
Surely someone endowed with a mind as powerful as yours can entertain me with an answer. There's no such thing as 'random'. The Universe is not serendipitous. Everything happens for a reason.

Geoff leans into the phone.

GEOFF
Did you kill her?

STRANGER
Her? Doesn't ring a bell.

GEOFF
You know who I'm talking about.

STRANGER
I believe we both know the answer to that question.
GEOFF
Why?

                    STRANGER
Because she was there. And it was exactly
what you wanted me to do.

The stranger hangs up.

INT. GEOFFREY'S LIVING ROOM - SAME

The sound of a dial tone filters through the
line. Geoff hangs up.

EXT. SIDEWALK - DAY

Geoff catches up to Livia who walks briskly
towards her apartment building.

                    GEOFF
Livia?

Geoff grabs her by the shoulder. Livia
nearly jumps out of her skin.

                    LIVIA
Jeez, what's wrong with you? Don't scare me
like that!

                    GEOFF
Sorry.

Livia turns to Geoff, face stressed.

                    LIVIA
What do you want?

                    GEOFF
There's something I need to tell you.

                    LIVIA
What is it?

                    GEOFF
I probably should have said something before
but...

                    LIVIA
What's wrong?

                    GEOFF
I don't want to put you or Josh in danger.

                    LIVIA
Why would you think Josh is in danger?

                    GEOFF
I've been getting phone calls.

In the distance Neal and Lee watch from an
unmarked squad car.

INT. LIVIA'S LIVING ROOM - LATER

Livia and Geoff sit across from each other.
Geoff sits on the couch. Livia sits in a
chair.

                    LIVIA
I'm confused. This guy believes you're God
and killed Monica? Why?

                    GEOFF
Bad timing. She was in the wrong place at
the wrong time. We're dealing with a
bonafide sociopath.

                    LIVIA
It doesn't make sense. There are millions of
people in the city. Hundreds traveling at
the time she was killed. There has to be a
connection. Something or someone tying us to
the killer.

                    GEOFF
Like you, I have more questions than answers.

                    LIVIA
You think he'll do something to hurt me and
Josh?

                    GEOFF
I don't know. Maybe Terence knew something...

                    LIVIA
Don't you dare blame my husband for this.

Livid stands and begins absently pacing the
room.

                    GEOFF
I'm sorry, Livia. I didn't mean it like
that...you're a beautiful woman. Maybe the
killer's infatuated with you. He got rid of
your husband, then got rid of Monica. She
was your support system. Now he's coming
after me.

                    LIVIA
God, I hope not.

Geoff and Livia hug.

INT. STRANGER'S LIVING ROOM - NIGHT

A COMPUTER SCREEN. A news article appears
with the caption "Man shot on subway" with a
small picture of Livia and Terence below.

INT. SUBWAY/FLASHBACK - NIGHT

A masked man using a chloroform drenched
towel steps out of the darkness and covers
Monica's nose and mouth from behind.

He drags her into a phone booth, which is
underneath an escalator out of public view.

The masked man grabs the phone and dials a
number with Monica leaning unconsciously
into his arms. The sound of the phone
ringing filters through the receiver.

He goes into his pocket bringing out a vial
and a tight wire. He wraps the wire around
Monica's neck then waves the vial under her
nose.

She slowly comes to and panics as a knife is
plunged into her chest.

The masked man and Monica struggle. Monica
reaches over her head and scratches him on
the neck. He goes into his pocket, pulls out
a large blade, and slams her hand against
the wall before cutting her fingers off with
the sharp blade in one furious swipe.

Monica screams as Geoff's voice filters
through the line.

                    GEOFF (ON PHONE)
Hello.

                    STRANGER (Into phone)
See what you made me do?

INT. GEOFFREY'S BEDROOM - SAME

Geoff is jarred out awake. He sits upright.

EXT. BROWNSTONE APARTMENT - DAY

Livia leaves the brownstone, locking the
door behind her. At the bottom of the
stairs, Geoff waits.

He looks casual, hands shoved into his
pockets. The sidewalk is busy as pedestrians
walk by in both directions. Livia, looking
surprised, takes her time walking down the
stairs towards Geoff.

                    LIVIA
I'm telling the police about the phone
calls.

Livia brushes by. Geoff grabs Livia by the
arm.

                    GEOFF
          (Panic)
Are you nuts? Don't do that.

                    LIVIA
Why?

                    GEOFF
He's talking. He's going to confess.

                    LIVIA
Good, then I'll have more information to
give the police. Did he tell you he killed
Monica and Terence?

                    GEOFF
Not yet. I'm working on him.

                    LIVIA
How many others is he going to kill before
you get what you need? It's not a game. I
don't trust you anymore.

Livia walks away. Geoff catches up, grabbing
her by the arm again. She turns, as if
coming to a realization.

                    LIVIA
Wait a second...you said something about the
subway.

                    GEOFF
What?

                    LIVIA
The night the detectives were in my apartment.
You said, the subway is a dangerous place at
night. How did you know about the subway? How
did you know she was killed at night?

Livia pulls out of Geoff's grasp and backs
away. He follows, grabbing her arm again.

                    GEOFF
What are you saying?

                    LIVIA
It makes sense. The phone calls. Terence.
Monica...

Geoff shakes her.

                    GEOFF
How could you say that? Terence was my
friend, that's the only reason I stick
around—I would never do anything to hurt you
or Josh. I happened to overhear the officers
when I was in Josh's room.

He lets her go, eyes hurt. Livia covers her
face with both of her hands.

                    LIVIA
You're right. I'm a mess. I don't know who
to trust anymore...not even myself. I don't
know if it's all in my head. Someone's
watching me and Josh. I feel like I'm losing
my mind. How could I think you'd...? Damn it,
Geoff. I'm sorry.

Geoff consoles Livia, wrapping an arm around
her shoulders.

The embrace ends.

                    LIVIA
I'm telling the detectives about the calls.
If I don't, he might kill you next. Forgive
me, I have to go.

                    GEOFF
He won't. Don't do it, Liv!

Geoff starts out after Livia but an unmarked police
car with Detective Neal and Lee inside pulls to the
curb and cuts him off. Livia breaks into a stride,
disappearing into a crowd of pedestrians as she
crosses the street.

Detective Lee smiles at Geoff, follows him
in the unmarked squad car.

                    LEE
Trouble in paradise?

                    GEOFF
We're in a rough spot.

                    NEAL
So you're dating?

                    GEOFF
Not exactly.

                    LEE
What exactly do you call it? Shacking up?

                    GEOFF
It's not like that-

                    NEAL
But you want it to be, don't you?

Geoff's hand crumples into a fist. He glares at
Detective Neal.

                    GEOFF
Go fuck yourself!

                    LEE
Ooo temper temper! Did I touch a nerve?

                    NEAL
We're just doing our investigation. Nothing
personal.

                    GEOFF
I don't give a shit about your investigation
so back the fuck off and leave us alone!

                    LEE
We'll be in touch, Mr. Davis.

The unmarked squad car drives away.

INT. LIVIA'S KITCHEN - NIGHT

Livia washes a dish and puts it into a
nearby dish drainer.

She hangs her kitchen towel on the sink then
opens the refrigerator, but is started by a
loud noise.

Livia leaves the refrigerator door open and
drifts out of the room.

INT. LIVIA'S LIVING ROOM - CONTINUE

The stranger, wearing a black ski mask
appears and grabs Livia from behind.

A violent struggle ensues with Livia
knocking over a lamp as they bang into a
picture hanging on the wall. The picture
shatters and falls, prompting Josh to run
into the room.

Livia digs her finger nails into the
attacker's neck, leaving a long gaping
scratch and a trail of blood. Struggling to
free herself from his grasp, Livia kicks,
knocking over a lamp, also shattering it.

                JOSH(OS)
              (Screaming)
Mommy!

The attacker throws Livia to the floor. She
grabs a piece of glass from the cracked
painting and stabs the attacker in the foot,
leaving a long bloody gash in his boot. The
attacker growls and screams.

She scrambles to her feet. In a rage, the
attacker grabs Livia and throws her through
the living room window. The window shatters.

EXT. BROWNSTONE - CONTINUE

Livia lies face down on the lawn in a pile
of broken glass. Cuts and bruises mark her
arms, face, and legs. She moves slowly,
weakly pulling herself to her feet.

                JOSH
Mommy!

Livia looks over her shoulder. The attacker
and Josh stand one story up, looking down at
her from out of her shattered apartment
window. The attacker dangles Josh under his
arm like a football.

                JOSH
MOMMMY!

The attacker leaves the window, taking Josh with him.

                    LIVIA
No! You can't.

Livia pulls herself to her feet and drags her body up the stairs. The entry door is locked. A young woman pulls the door open.

Livia limps into the building in pursuit.

INT. LIVIA'S LIVING ROOM - CONTINUE

Livia hobbles through the apartment, bare feet crunching down on shards of glass.

                    LIVIA
Josh! Baby where are you?

Outside, an ambulance siren sounds and lights from a police car flash manically against the walls.

Livia finds a note on the table.

                    LIVIA
                  (Reading)
Talk to the police and the boy dies.

Livia crumples the paper in her hand then faints.

Detective Neal walks in. He is followed by his partner Lee. They help Livia to her feet.

82

                    LIVIA
He took Josh.

Livia falls into Neal's shoulder, sobbing
loudly.

                    NEAL
You know who took him?

                    LIVIA
              (Sobbing)
If I fucking knew who had him, I wouldn't be
terrified right now.

                    LEE
Looks like you had quite a fall.

                    LIVIA
I was in the kitchen washing dishes when I
heard a noise. I walked into the living room
and he lunged at me.

                    NEAL
No sign of forced entry. The locks are
intact.

                    LIVIA
He had a fucking key. Whoever it was, walked
right in and stole my son.

                    LEE
Does the father have any living relatives?
Someone who might want custody of Josh, or
visitation? Any court issues?

                    LIVIA
Josh has relatives but they can see him any
time they want. We have a good relationship.
They would never do something like this.

                    NEAL
Any messages from the kidnapper?

Livia looks to the floor in fear.

                    LEE
We can't save your son if you don't tell us
everything you know.

                    LIVIA
I can't.

                    NEAL
Why?

                    LIVIA
He'll kill him.

                    LEE
We need officers out there looking for the
kid now.

                    NEAL
I'm already on it.

Geoff limps in, looking slightly frazzled
and out of breath.

                    GEOFF
Livia? You okay?

                    LIVIA
Josh is gone. How did you?

                    GEOFF
I was on my way over. I was hoping we could
finish our conversation.

                    LIVIA
He took Josh.

                    GEOFF
Fuck.

Geoff pounds the wall with his fist.

                    LEE
Pipe down or I'm putting you in handcuffs.

Geoff calms down, glares at Detective Lee.

                    GEOFF
I'm upset. How else do you expect me to
react?

                    LEE
Let us do our jobs. We'll find Josh.

                    LIVIA
If you were doing your damn job you'd have
this maniac by now.

Lee goes toward the door.

                    LEE
I'll find your son. You have my word.

EXT. ABANDONED BUILDING/ROOM - NIGHT

Josh, wearing a pair of pajamas sits gagged
and bound to a wooden chair in the middle of
a dark, dank room. A leaky pipe drips into a
pool of stagnant water. A rat scurries
across the floor close to Josh's feet.

Josh struggles to wriggle himself free, but tips his chair over landing into a grimy pool of water. He lets out a muffled scream.

Gazing up, he sees a shiny object aimed toward the door. A rope tied to a pendulum hanging from the ceiling is rigged to swing towards the door when opened. Josh struggles until he wriggles himself free, then unties the rope binding his feet.

He climbs into a curtain-less window and stares down at the street below. Josh tries to open the window but the window won't budge.

He uses the chair to hoist himself to the top of the window where he unlocks it. He looks down. There's a fire escape.

EXT. ABANDONED BUILDING - SAME

Below, a car parks next to the building. The driver's face is concealed by a shadow in the darkened car. The headlights flicker off.

INT. ABANDONED BUILDING/ROOM - SAME

Josh ducks out of sight, stooping below the window out of the driver's view just as the loud sound of a car door opening and closing shatters the night's quiet.

Josh stands. He looks toward the door.

                    LEE (VO)
JOSH? You in here?

                    JOSH
I'm in here!!

                    LEE (VO)
               (Sounding closer)
KEEP YELLING SO I CAN FIND YOU.

                    JOSH
I'm over here but don't come in! You'll get
hurt.

                    LEE (OS)
          (Voice filtering through door)
I'm right here Josh, I'm coming in.

                    JOSH
Don't! You'll get killed!

INT. ABANDONED BUILDING/HALLWAY - SAME

Gun in hand, Lee takes a step back then
hurls himself shoulder first into the door.

INT. ABANDONED BUILDING/ROOM - SAME

Josh covers his eyes with both hands and
GASPS.

The rope over the door snaps. The pendulum
falls, landing right into Lee's chest. He
falls to floor, blood turning his shirt dark
red.

Josh scurries past Lee's body with both
hands over his eyes, and goes out of the
door.

                    LEE
              (Weakly)
Josh...get to the car. Use the radio and
call for help.

A thin line of blood trickles from Lee's
mouth.

                    JOSH
Yes, sir...

EXT. ABANDONED BUILDING - LATER

Josh stands next to Lee's dark blue unmarked
police car. He opens the door. Inside is a
computer screen and a police radio. Josh
presses a button.

                    JOSH
              (Into walkie-talkie)
Hello? The policeman got hurt. Is anybody
out there?

                    DISPATCHER (OS-Walkie)
Roger that. Do you know where you are?

                    JOSH
           (Into walkie talkie)
He's hurt.

                    DISPATCHER (OS-Walkie)
Can you give me an address?

                    JOSH
              (Into walkie-talkie)
Nobody lives in the building. It doesn't
have an address. Please hurry the killer is
coming back.

Josh hides under the steering wheel as a car parks behind him. At the sound of the car door opening and closing, Josh catches his breath and draws further into the darkness of the car.

The attacker's shoes crunch down on the gravelly sidewalk, step after step as it reaches Lee's car. Josh stares nervously at the walkie-talkie.

After thirty seconds of agonizing silence, the attacker walks away and Josh goes undetected.

The boy sticks his head up. The other car is still parked behind him.

                    DISPATCHER
              (From walkie-talkie)
Hello? Anybody there?

Josh opens the car door and runs away.

EXT. SIDEWALK - LATER

The street is dark and the sidewalk is damp. Josh peddles his legs as fast as he can.

From the side of a rundown apartment building a stray dog enters the sidewalk. After relieving himself at a nearby garbage can, the dog finds Josh and befriends him, nuzzling Josh's hand with his wet nose.

                    JOSH
  Hey there pup.

A shadow looms behind them. An elderly woman with stringy silvery hair grabs the dog by his tail and pulls him away from Josh.
The dog yelps loudly. Josh stares wide eyed innocence at the woman.

                    OLD WOMAN
What are you doing out here so late? Ain't you got a home to go to?

                    JOSH
I'm lost.

                    OLD WOMAN
Where's your mama?

                    JOSH
I don't know.

INT. GEOFFREY'S LIVING ROOM - SAME

Livia pushes the door open, albeit cautiously, and walks into Geoff's apartment.

                    LIVIA
Geoff?

Papers lay scattered across a coffee table that sits in the middle of the room. His typewriter has been dumped upside down onto the floor.

The rest of the apartment has been ransacked. Livia closes the door behind her.

                    LIVIA
Geoff?

The apartment is silent, save for the sound of a faucet dripping.

Livia sees the phone. She lifts the receiver and puts it close to her ear. The phone is dead.

Livia follows the cord and sees that the wires have been ripped from the wall.

She drops the phone and lifts a sheet of paper from the table and turns it over. A manuscript.

A shadowy figure appears behind her. Before she can turn around, he grabs her by the hair and flings her to the floor. Livia screams.

She rolls on her back and finds the stranger standing over her, a mask covering his face. She kicks him then scrambles away, cowering on the side of the coffee table.

                    LIVIA
What did you do with Josh?

The stranger throws the coffee table aside and reaches for Livia, grabbing her by the ankle and pulling her towards him.

Livia kicks the stranger in the groin with her other foot. He bends over, reeling in pain.

Livia scrambles to her feet, grabs a lamp, and cracks him over the head. The room goes dark.

                    LIVIA
What did you do with my son?

The stranger falls on his side. Livia holds
the lamp over her head, close to cracking
him with it again. The stranger opens his
eyes, holding Livia's gaze as she finally
swings the lamp.

He catches it mid-air and grabs her by the
arm.

The stranger flips Livia over. She lands
opposite of him on the floor.

The stranger scrambles his feet quickly, out
of breath, but ready for a fight. Livia
crawls behind the couch. The stranger pulls
the sofa and flips it over.

Livia scrambles to her feet and races for
the door. The stranger jumps over the sofa.

She opens the door, but not fast enough to
get out. He slams it closed, forcing her
back against the door.

                    LIVIA
What did you do with Josh?

The stranger stares at her, slightly confused
for a moment then gets close enough to blow
his breath in her face.

Livia knees the stranger in the groin. He
falls back as she escapes.

EXT. SIDEWALK - LATER

The old woman and Josh walk down the street.

                    OLD WOMAN
I suppose I ought to keep you till somebody
offers a reward. But I guess the best thing
to do is get you home to your mama.

Josh nods.

                    OLD WOMAN
I saw a picture of you on the news. 'Cute
kid' I said. I suppose your mama will be the
happiest woman on Earth when she sees your
face.

INT. GEOFFREY'S LIVING ROOM - LATER

Geoff walks in, finding his apartment
ransacked. Livia's purse is on the floor.

A shadow lurks behind him in the darkness.
Geoff finds the pages of his manuscript and
begins putting them in order.

A hand sneaks from behind and covers his
mouth. A blade is pressed against his neck.

                    STRANGER
You disappoint me.
Geoff pulls the stranger's hand away.

                    GEOFF
How did you get in?

                    STRANGER
I have my ways. How's your book?

                         GEOFF
So you read my manuscript? Did you like it?

                        STRANGER
Soliciting the unqualified opinion of a
serial killer? Not too bright, are you?
Perhaps you might ask your friend, Livia.

                         GEOFF
I did. Two years ago.

                        STRANGER
And?

                         GEOFF
And she hated it. I submitted the book under
a pseudonym. I wanted to impress her.

                        STRANGER
Interesting… it seems truth is much stranger
than fiction.

                         GEOFF
What do you mean?

                        STRANGER
You had this planned from the beginning.
Unfortunately I'm not just a character
in your book. I'm real. Which means the
story doesn't end the way you want it to
end.
                         GEOFF
How so?

                        STRANGER
In my version...you die. It would feel a
little contrived to end it any other way.

Geoff leans close to the Stranger's ear.

                         GEOFF
You're not writing the story.

                       STRANGER
I'm an obstacle sandwiched between the
protagonist and the victim. The same
obstacle that will ultimately bring them
together I suppose. Call me cynical, Isn't
this just a tad cliché. Too bad you didn't
have the guts to tell her who really killed
her husband.

EXT. SUBWAY/FLASHBACK - NIGHT

Terence Thorton waits for a train in an
empty subway station where Geoff can be seen
lurking in the shadows under the stairwell.

The 'B' train goes by without stopping.
Terence checks his watch. The time is "1:30
a.m." An exit sign begins to buzz and
flicker out.

Terence turns to find Geoff standing behind
him, a gun pointing at his face.

                       TERENCE
What are you doing?

                         GEOFF
Don't make this harder than it already is.
Get over there.

Geoff points to a nearby phone booth with
the end of his gun. Terence backs away.

                       TERENCE
Why are you doing this?

Geoff shoots him in the stomach. Terence stumbles into a phone booth and falls on his back, cracking the glass behind him.

Geoff watches as Terence chokes on his own blood.

                    TERENCE
              (gurgling)
Why?

The A train arrives. Geoff gets on board, watching Terence die as the train pulls away.

END FLASHBACK

INT. GEOFFREY'S LIVING ROOM - PRESENT DAY

The stranger flashes the shiny knife at Geoff.

                    STRANGER
Which brings me to my original question...You ruined a man's life. Why?

The stranger punches Geoff. He falls to the floor with the stranger crushing down on top of him.
                    GEOFF
Because of her. She told me the characters needed to be real for the story to work. So I started over. Using real people in my book. Nothing I wrote was ever good enough for Livia. I was never good enough.

                    STRANGER
She was married. But you were in love with
her, weren't you? That's why you off'd the
husband. You wanted to ruin her perfect
life. Your so called *infatuation* with Carla
was just a ruse so no one would suspect it
was you. What about me? Where do I fit in? A
convenient scapegoat for your crimes?

                    GEOFF
I didn't pick you. You picked me.

                    STRANGER
Ah. Yes. The phone book.

                    GEOFF
You chose me.

Geoff squirms under the stranger's weight.

                    STRANGER
You're right. I did. After I found your
number I wrote your address down. I followed
you and watched you following her. Hiding in
the shadows...*stalking* her, you sick fuck.

                    GEOFF
You're fucking delusional.

                    STRANGER
Am I? So tell me. Does she die?

                    GEOFF
I don't know. You're the killer. You tell
me.

                    STRANGER

You're the writer. I'm just a character in
your fucking universe. You're god. You tell
me how it ends and I obey. Does she live or
does she die?

The stranger flashes the side of the knife.

                    GEOFF

She lives.

The stranger laughs, falling backwards onto
the floor. Geoff pulls himself to his feet,
kicking the stranger as he gets up.

                    STRANGER

What about the little boy?

                    GEOFF

He'll live. The readers deserve a happy
ending, don't they?

                    STRANGER

I'm interested in seeing where this goes.
But rest assured, you haven't gotten away.
Judgment will come, and when it does, it
will be by my hands.

The stranger walks out.

Geoff sits sifts through the pages of his
manuscript.

He comes to the title sheet which reads "A
murder in Capetown by Geoffrey Oliver
Davis".

Geoff rearranges the manuscript then lays it
back on the table.

After standing the sofa upright, Geoff finds
his typewriter and places it on the desk.

A single sheet of paper falls to the floor.
The title page reads "What Dreams Become" by
Sam Houston.

Geoff tears the manuscript in half and drops
it in the wastebasket. He goes into his desk
and finds the rest of the manuscript. It is
covered in red markings, with notes from
Livia Thorton.

Geoff dumps the rest of his old manuscript
in the garbage.

INT. ABANDONED BUILDING - LATER

Lee lies on his back, seemingly unconscious.
The stalker walks in, a mask covering his
face. Lee watches as he tip toes by.

He draws his pistol and aims at the stalker.

                LEE
Take another step and I'll blow your brains
all over the fucking wall.

The stalker stops cold.

                LEE
 Put your hands over your head.

The stalker reluctantly complies.

                LEE
Take off your mask...slowly. And don't try
anything funny, dipshit.

The stalker pulls the mask off of his face and throws it at Lee. The masks lands on Lee's head and in a blur the stalker is gone.

                    LEE
Fuck.

In frustration, Lee fires a shot at the ceiling releasing a huge piece of plaster which falls on top of his debilitated body.

                    LEE
              (Muffled)
Shit. I'm done.

INT. OLD WOMAN'S APARTMENT - NIGHT

Clutter overwhelms the old woman's tiny apartment. Boxes of cat litter sits in the corner and newspapers line the floor.

                  OLD WOMAN
I'm trying to get my kitty potty trained, don't mind the paper.

Josh sits on the couch.

                  OLD WOMAN
Are you hungry?

                    JOSH
Yes.

                  OLD WOMAN
I would imagine so after the night you've had.

The old woman offers a wry smile then heads into the kitchen. Josh watches from the couch as she prepares a bowl of cereal.

                    OLD WOMAN
I hope you like cereal. Most kids do.

The old woman pours a table spoon of anti-freeze into the bowl.

She brings it to Josh.

                    OLD WOMAN
Enjoy...

The woman offers him a witch-like grin. Josh puts the spoon close to his mouth.

                    JOSH
May I have a glass of water?

                    OLD WOMAN
Sure...

The woman goes into the kitchen. Josh slips out the front door.

EXT. CITY STREET - NIGHT

Josh runs away.

EXT. CITY STREET - SAME

Geoff races down the sidewalk.

                    GEOFF
Josh! Where are you?

EXT. CITY STREET - SAME

Livia scours the street aimlessly in search
of Josh. A woman passes by.

                    LIVIA
Excuse me, ma'am, have you seen this little
boy?

Livia shows the woman a picture of Josh. The
woman shakes her head and walks away.

                    LIVIA
This is bullshit, somebody saw something.

An unmarked police car pulls to the curb
next to Livia. Detective Neal is inside.

                    NEAL
They found Josh.

                    LIVIA
Is he okay?

                    NEAL
He got away. My partner was injured and is
on his way to the hospital. But the good
news is Josh is still alive. The bad news,
is he ran away when the killer came back.

                    LIVIA
So he's okay?

                    NEAL
Not if the killer finds him first. Lee found
him on 23rd and Roosevelt.

                    LIVIA
Then he's close.

                    NEAL
Between you and me...when I find the bastard
who did this, I'm going to rip his fucking
heart out.

                    LIVIA
Not if I get there first. I'll tear down
every goddam building in this neighborhood
if I have to.

Neal drives away.

EXT. CITY STREET - LATER

Josh walks slowly down the sidewalk. Geoff
spots him from behind.

                    GEOFF
Josh!

Josh turns and sees Geoff. He runs.

                    GEOFF
Josh it's okay! Come back.

A few paces ahead, Livia races across the
street. Josh sees his mother and runs toward
her, darting from the sidewalk.
The headlights of a parked car are turned
on. The tires squeal as the car revs up and
speeds toward Josh.

Geoff sees the car, races from the sidewalk
towards Josh and is hit by the speeding
vehicle. The stranger, who is behind the
wheel drives away at an even faster speed.

Geoff is thrown to the side of the road into
a pile of rubble and lands on a rod,
impaling his shoulder.

Livia and Josh race to each other and hug
but sees that Geoff is injured nearby.

They race towards him. Livia kneels by his
side.

                    LIVIA
You saved my baby! Thank you a thousand times!
Don't worry, you're gonna be all right.

Geoff squirms. Livia holds his legs.

                    LIVIA
Be still, you might damage something.

                    GEOFF
You sound like a nurse. What can't you do?

Geoff offers Livia a weak smile in spite of
his obvious pain.

                    LIVIA
I can't laugh. I'm too scared. Livia tries
to hold Geoff's legs in place and notices a
large gash across the top of his boot.

                    LIVIA
                  (Stunned)
What happened to your shoe?

Geoff falls unconscious.

INT. BRITTINGHAM PUBLISHING OFFICE - DAY

Livia stands in her cube. The walls are bare, all of her artwork removed. A packed box sits on top of her desk.

Carla, the pretty brunette stands nearby.

                    CARLA
We're gonna miss you Liv.

                    LIVIA
Well come around here and give me a hug. I'm gonna miss you too.

Carla and Livia hug.

                    CARLA
Who's going to give me advice when I have boyfriend problems?

                    LIVIA
You can call me whenever you want. In fact, promise you'll visit next Christmas.

                    CARLA
Girl, you know I'm Jewish. By the way, you hear about Geoff?
Louis said his book is on the New York Best Seller's list. I tried calling to congratulate him, but he's not answering the phone.

                    LIVIA
                 (Quietly)
Yeah, I hear it's flying off the shelves. He wrote it rather quickly. A best seller in six months is quite an accomplishment.
                    CARLA

Hmm...I thought you'd be happy for him.

                    LIVIA
Happy for what? That he stole parts of my
life for a book?

                    CARLA
You gave him your blessing. What happened to
the killer?

                    LIVIA
He's still out there...somewhere.

Livia takes a sip from the coffee cup.

                    CARLA
So...looking forward to life in Minnes-

                    LIVIA
Carla-

Geoff appears, limping slightly, and shifting
his weight to a cane he uses to get around.

                    CARLA
I guess you two have things to talk about.
                 (To Geoff)
Stop by my cubicle before when you get a
chance.

Carla gives Livia a sly smile; winks at
Geoff, then walks away.

                    GEOFF
I know you don't want to see it. But I
brought a copy of the book.

                    LIVIA
Why?

                    GEOFF
I think you should read it. It's about you.
It's about what happened to us.

                    LIVIA
I have nightmares to remind me, no need to
see it detailed in a novel.

                    GEOFF
I understand. At least read the dedication.

Geoff opens the book and hands it to Livia.

Livia reluctantly takes the book and reads
the passage.

                    LIVIA
It's beautiful. Thank you for the kind
words. I'm sure Terence would thank you too.
If he could.

                    GEOFF
I wanted you to see it. The book is yours to
read when you're ready. I even signed it.

Geoff pulls Livia into a friendly embrace.

                    GEOFF
Have a fun move. I hope things are good for
you.

They hug. Livia sees healed scars on Geoff's
neck.

INTERCUT: INT.LIVIA'S LIVING ROOM/GEOFFREY'S
CUBICLE @ BRITTINGHAM - NIGHT

Livia sits in a chair, her legs curled
beneath her comfortably, as she reads a
book.

The phone RINGS...second ring...third ring.
Finally, she answers.

                    LIVIA
               (Into phone)
Hello?

                    GEOFF
               (Into phone)
You're still here.

                    LIVIA
               (Into phone)
I leave tomorrow.

                    GEOFF
               (Into phone)
I thought you were leaving for Minnesota
today?
                    LIVIA
               (Into phone)
There's been a change of plans.

                    GEOFF
               (Into phone)
I wish I had known earlier. I would have
taken you out to dinner.

                    LIVIA
               (Into phone)
I'm not hungry.

                    GEOFF
                 (Into phone)
Is something wrong? You sound upset.

                    LIVIA
                 (Into phone)
I was reading your book.

                    GEOFF
                 (Into phone)
What did you think?

                    LIVIA
                 (Into phone)
The writing is familiar. Like something I've
read before.

                    GEOFF
                 (Into phone)
We come across a lot of writers in this
business. That shouldn't come as a surprise
to you.

                    LIVIA
                 (Into phone)
How did you know I was moving to Minnesota?
                    GEOFF
                 (Into phone)
You told me.

                    LIVIA
                 (Into phone)
I never told you.

                    GEOFF
                 (Into phone)
Okay, you caught me. I confess...

INT. CLASSY RESTAURANT/FLASHBACK - NIGHT

Carla, wearing a nice dress sits at a small
table with a view of the city's skyline.
Geoff joins Carla, sitting across from her
on the other side of the table.

                    CARLA
You made quite a turnaround. You're
confident. Sexy...I like that.

                    GEOFF
Thank you...Success has a way of changing a
man. Helps him see the value in himself.

                    CARLA
I agree.

Carla smiles beautifully at Geoff. A waiter
arrives at the table and pours wine.

INTERCUT: INT. LIVIA'S LIVING ROOM/GEOFFREY'S
CUBICLE @ BRITTINGHAM

PRESENT DAY

Livia coils the phone cord around her
fingers and looks solemnly at her feet.

                    GEOFF
              (Into phone, laughs)
I sort of *strangled* it out of Carla tonight.
Don't be upset with her. She was under the
impression that I already knew.

                    LIVIA
              (Into phone)
Why?

                    GEOFF
                (Into phone)
Why not? You didn't want me to know?

                    LIVIA
                (Into phone)
I tried calling you at home a few times but
didn't get an answer. The killer is still
out there.

                    GEOFF
                (Into phone)
When you get to the end of the book, you'll
see that the detectives already who he is.
It's just a matter of finding him. He's not
going to bother you anymore. You're safe.

                    LIVIA
                (Into phone)
If it's one thing I've learned from this… no
one is truly safe and to trust no one.
                    GEOFF
                (Into phone)
What's that supposed to mean?

                    LIVIA
                (Into phone)
I'm sure you know...I have to go. I have a
long trip tomorrow and I really need to get
some rest. Goodbye Geoff.

                    GEOFF
                (Into phone)
Wait-

                    LIVIA
                (Into phone)
What?

                    GEOFF
                (Into phone)
I miss you already.

Livia holds the phone and listens to the
sound of Geoff's breathing.

                    LIVIA
                (Into phone)
That night...your boot-

                    GEOFF
                (Into phone)
I'd just been hit by a speeding car. What
did you expect? My shoes to be in perfect
condition?

Livia holds the phone.

                    GEOFF
I'm sure you have to get some rest. So guess
I'll have to let you go. For now.

                    LIVIA
                (Into phone)
Goodbye Geoff.

                    GEOFF
                (Into phone)
No goodbyes. Goodbye sounds so permanent.
We'll see each other again.

                    LIVIA
                (Into phone)
Hopefully under better circumstances. Take
care.

Livia hangs up. She stares at the phone.

Josh walks in.

                    JOSH
Mommy? Is it time to go yet?

Livia looks out the window.

                    LIVIA
Yeah. Our ride is here now.

                    JOSH
Mommy, why did say we were leaving tomorrow?

                    LIVIA
I'm sorry baby, you're right. I did tell a
lie. I won't do it again. Okay?

                    JOSH
Why?

                    LIVIA
Josh, get your bag. We'll talk about it on
the way to California. Ready for some warm
weather?

INT. GEOFFREY'S BEDROOM - NIGHT

Geoff sleeps.

The phone RINGS...second ring...third ring.

Geoff answers.

                    GEOFF
Hello?

                    STRANGER (ON PHONE)
Exciting isn't it?

                    GEOFF
               (Into phone)
If this is your idea of excitement. They're
going to catch you.

                STRANGER (ON PHONE)
And I'll be arrested for your crimes.

                    GEOFF
               (Into phone)
You killed the girl.

                STRANGER (ON PHONE)
You killed her husband. And for what? A
bestselling novel? You're pathetic. You must
lead a very empty life.

                    GEOFF
               (Into phone)
I'm happy now. In the end, that's all that
matters.

                STRANGER (ON PHONE)
               (Laughing)
Let's play a game...suppose I have a murder
weapon. Let's suppose your clever little
hiding place wasn't so clever and I have it.
While you were away, I made myself at home
in your apartment. It was cozy. Warm...

Geoff throws the phone down.

INT. BATHROOM - CONTINUE

Geoff pulls the mirror out of the wall.
Inside is a ring, a stack of paper, and a
small steel case. Geoff opens the case and
finds nothing inside.

                    STRANGER (VO)
I know exactly how you think. I'm YOUR god.

INT. GEOFFREY'S BEDROOM - CONTINUE

Geoff puts the receiver close to his ear.

                    STRANGER (ON PHONE)
When they find out you're the one who killed
Terence, they'll put two and two together.
They'll know you killed her too.

                    GEOFF
               (Into phone)
I didn't kill her fuckwad. You did.

                    STRANGER (ON PHONE)
Did I?

The stranger hangs up.

                    GEOFF
...HELLO? HELLO?

DIAL TONE.

Geoff smashes the phone into the cradle and
follows the wire with his eyes across the
table, along the floor, over the recliner,
to the wall. The wires were already ripped
from the jack.

A look of realization crosses his face. The
phone was never connected.

Geoff slides to the floor, pulling his knees
to his chest.

FADE OUT

www.ingramcontent.com/pod-product-compliance
Lightning Source LLC
Chambersburg PA
CBHW021204110726
47900CB00002B/724